The Blue Hair Club

From the "Godfather Tales" Series

**By
Dan Lauria
&
Cathryn Farnsworth**

Illustrated by Brandon Morino

The Blue Hair Club: And Other Stories
Copyright © 2013 Dan Lauria and Cathryn Farnsworth

ISBN-13: 978-0615859248
ISBN-10: 0615859240

For inquiries, please visit:
www.thegodfathertales.com

Written by
Dan Lauria
and Cathryn Farnsworth

Illustrations by
Brandon Morino

The Godfather Tales

When I chose Dan to be my son's godfather, I knew he would be a good choice. However, I had no idea how amazing his relationship with my son Julian would become, and how devoted Dan would be in that role!

Story telling is a big part of my parenting. Dan took it to another level and started creating stories nearly everyday. Once that began, Julian only wanted original tales for story time. Each day would begin with, "Surely you know the story of the little boy who fell through the hole in his sock, don't you?" Julian would protest, "That's not a real story!!", and Dan would have all day to come up with the story -- thus began the "Godfather Tales".

I hope your family gets as much joy out of them as ours did in creating them.

Cathryn Farnsworth

THE BLUE HAIR CLUB

Once there was a golden-haired
boy named Julian.

Julian had lots of friends.

One of Julian's friends was named Jack.
Jack was new at school and very shy.

One day, the school bully knocked some books out of Jack's hands and made fun of him.

Julian stepped in and helped Jack by picking up his books.

The bully started making fun of Julian...
... but Julian just walked away.

At bedtime, he told his mom what happened.

"This boy picked on Jack and me at school, and I did what you said to do. No matter what he did, I didn't get mad or throw a fit. I just walked away."

"That was very good of you," his mom said. "Bullies are usually people who have been picked on themselves and are hurting inside - or they are wanting attention so they get it whatever way they can. You aren't going to change a bully by fighting back."

"Thanks, Mom, I know you're right - but I sure wish I could have punched him in the nose!!"

The next morning his mom came into Julian's room to wake him up - and she was startled by what she saw.

"Ahhhhh!!! What did you DO to your HAIR??!", she exclaimed.

AAAAAAA
AARRRRR
GGGGGHH
HHHHHH!!!!

Julian rushed into the bathroom and looked
in the mirror.

CLICK!!

13

Blue hair!!! A whole head
of BLUE HAIR!!!

"Aaaaaahhhhhhh!!!"

His father came in asking, "What's going on? We are going to be late for school". When he saw Julian's hair he shouted, "YIKES! WHAT DID YOU DO TO YOUR HAIR, BOY??!"

"I didn't do anything to it- it's just blue!"

His dad said, "Mom, we'd better shampoo his hair. We can't send him to school like that."

So they washed and washed and washed his head - they even used TURPENTINE - and guess what?

His hair stayed blue! So Julian's mom decided, "It's time to go to the Doctor!"

SUPER-SIZED SUPER SHAMPOO

SUPER VAC

TURPENTINE

CAR WASH ENTER

17

The other kids in the waiting room started making fun of him.

"Whoa, look at that silly boy with blue hair! Ha! You look ridiculous!"

"What did you do to your hair?!"

A little girl with no hair scooted closer to Julian and said, "I think your blue hair looks very nice."

Julian smiled. "Thank you. Don't you worry, you'll get hair back one day, too."

The girl said, "You're very nice." "You're very nice, too," Julian said.

Julian went into the exam room to see the doctor.
The doctor checked him carefully, and decided, "This
is not dye, this is not crayon, this is not paint. The boy
just has blue hair and I don't know why. But there's
nothing wrong with him."

While they were still in the exam room, they heard a big commotion coming from the waiting room. The exam room door BURST open, and when it did they saw....

...the girl's hair grew!

And it was blue, too!!!

She turned to Julian and said, "Thank you!"

The doctor checked her right away, and guess what?

She wasn't sick anymore!

The next day, even though Julian still had blue hair, he had to go back to school. Except now he was actually starting to LIKE his blue hair.

Everyone - even his friends - all pointed and laughed at him. They shouted, "Look at Julian, he's got blue hair!!!"

Well, the bully that had picked on him and his friend two days earlier stepped in and said, "Hey! Don't pick on HIM! I like this kid!"

And guess what happened to the bully? HIS hair turned BLUE! Everyone yelled, "Whoa! Wow! Now YOUR hair is blue!"

And the bully cheered, "Hey! We're the Blue Hair Club! Don't pick on him, and don't pick on me. Be nice."

The teacher came out and said, "Everyone settle down. I see these two boys have blue hair - and I think it's beautiful!"

Just then, the teacher's hair turned blue. Pretty quickly after that, everybody wanted blue hair because only NICE people had blue hair.

So, when somebody looks different than you, don't make fun of them because someday you might hope to be just as different as they are!

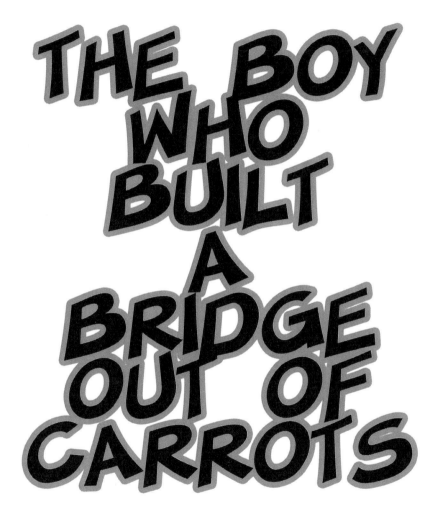

THE BOY WHO BUILT A BRIDGE OUT OF CARROTS

Once upon a time, long ago, there was a farming village by a river. The people in the village lived in houses made of mud.

There was one peculiar fact about this farming village - carrots were the only thing that would grow there!

All the boys and girls would work in their families' farms growing carrots. There were SO many carrots, that when they went to sell the carrots, they couldn't make much money, because carrots were all everyone ELSE had to sell.

On the other side of the river, there were NO carrots. So, one of the farmers asked, "Why don't we build a bridge so we can sell our carrots on the other side of the river?"

Everyone wondered, "Build a bridge out of what? There are no trees. It's just farms and miles and miles of carrots and dirt."

In this town, there was a little boy, and his name was Roscoe. And Roscoe said...

"Well, why can't we build a bridge out of carrots?"

They laughed and laughed and laughed at him, teasing, "Roscoe, you can't build a bridge out of carrots!!"

Roscoe said, "Well, that's ALL we have -- CARROTS!"
They said, "Roscoe, you're so dumb. You can't build a
bridge out of carrots."

They laughed at Roscoe, so Roscoe decided, "I'M going
to build a bridge out of carrots!"

So he dragged a whole load of carrots...

...and he put them in the river.

But the river just washed all of the carrots away!

All of the townspeople laughed at him.

"Ha ha ha, Roscoe! We said you can't build a bridge out of carrots!

What a waste of time and energy! You could have sold your carrots and made some money".

Roscoe said, "Yeah, well I tried. All we have are carrots! There's GOT to be a way to build a bridge out of carrots!"

Roscoe went back to pick more carrots, determined to find a way to build a bridge.

As he was packing a new batch of carrots into bags, he thought...

"Wait a minute!!!... What if I leave all of the carrots IN the bag, and put the BAG in the river??"

With his BAGS of carrots
Roscoe headed, once again,
to the river. He put one
bag of carrots in the river
and it didn't float away...

He put TWO bags of carrots
into the river, and THEY
didn't float away!!

And then THREE bags of
carrots, and it wasn't long
before...

He had built a bridge out of carrots!

The villagers ran to the river and asked, "Roscoe, how did you DO that?"

Roscoe beamed with pride. The villagers could now sell their carrots to the townspeople on the other side.

Incidentally, Roscoe became the richest kid around, because every time a villager crossed the bridge, they had to pay him 10 cents.

Roscoe did the best he could with what he had.... And that's the story of the boy who built a bridge out of carrots.

THE STORY OF THE SUN

Once upon a time, long, long, long, LONG ago, before there were any Julians around, or any cars, or any streets or roads - long before there was even the sun or the moon, there were just the animals.

But they couldn't see each other.

The hippo always stepped on the mouse's toe, and the mouse exclaimed, "Egad!! Can't you watch where you go?"

"I'm sorry, but I just can't see. There's no light", the hippo explained.

The giraffe bent down to get something to eat, and he banged his nose into the monkey's behind. And the monkey said, "What? What are you doing?!"

The giraffe said, "Oh, I'm sorry, I can't see."

It was then that the wise old owl flew way up to the highest point on the only tree. The owl hooted, "Hey, hey hey! All you animals. Over that mountain, I see a glow. It's a hot rock."

"Maybe if we had that rock over
here, we could see each other."

So the turtle, who was the FASTEST of all of the animals - faster than the cheetah, faster than any animal there EVER was - said, "I'm gonna RUN over there and check it out!"

ZOOOOOOOOOOOOOO

Well, that turtle ran over the mountain, saw the burning hot rock, and exclaimed, "Wow wow! I can see! I've got to bring this back to my friends so THEY can see, too!".

OOM!!

But the rock was so HOT, he couldn't touch it.

"Hmmm... Oh, I've got an idea!!"

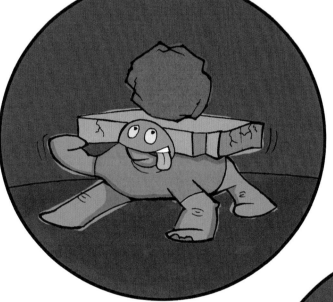

He maneuvered the hot rock onto a thick, flat rock. He then crawled under the thick, flat rock and slowly started to carry the big, hot rock back.

When he got to the top of the hill, the hot rock burned right through the flat rock, and started BURNING HIS BACK! He struggled to remove the hot rock as fast as possible, and finally it rolled off.

He came back to the other animals VERY slowly, with the rock melted over him, and they said, "Turtle! What happened to you? How come you're moving so slow, and what's that on your back?".

And he replied, "The hot rock the owl saw melted a flat rock onto my back!".

That is why all turtles to this day have shells and move s-l-o-w-l-y.

Well, the armadillo said, "Hey, I know what!
I have the longest tail of all of the animals.
I'll go over and wrap the hot rock up with
my tail and bring it back down the mountain".

So the armadillo went to the top of the
mountain. He saw the hot rock, and rolled
it onto his tail. He went, "Ow oww, ooooo
oooo oooo!" as he began dragging it down
the mountain. And he got about halfway
down the mountain...

...but he couldn't take it anymore! He tugged himself away from the hot rock. His long tail was gone - and all that was left was this skinny, scaly, shell-like tail.

And that's why all armadillos to this day have scaly, shell-like tails.

Well, the fox said, "I am tired of waiting for this hot rock! I'm going to go there and GRAB it in my mouth and BRING it down!"

The fox ran over, grabbed the rock and carried it the rest of the way down the mountain.

And everyone shouted, "Wahoo Mr. Fox! Way to go!"

When the fox jumped back, everyone said, "Hey, Mr. Fox. What happened to your mouth?" And the fox said, "The hot rock burned my mouth!"

And that's why, to this day, every fox you see has a black mouth.

All the animals were happy. Now they could see! Then the wise owl said, "You know, if we hung that rock in the sky, we could see a lot farther and we wouldn't have to stay near the rock to see".

"How are we going to get it up there?", the animals asked.

Well, the vulture, which was this big, huge, beautiful bird with the most gorgeous colorful feathers on his head, said, "I'll do it!"

So the vulture balanced the hot rock on his head, and he flew up into the sky. It got hotter and hotter and started to burn his head.

"I can do it! I can do it!", he said, and went higher and higher and higher and finally, he got way up there and hung the hot rock in the sky.

All of the beautiful feathers
on his head were gone, and
what remained was a bright
RED head.

And that's why all the vultures
to this day have no feathers on
their heads.

And that's also why when
you see vultures in the
desert, they're circling the
sun in the sky.

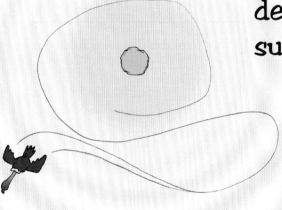

All the animals cheered and celebrated- they could finally see!

Many animals had been changed forever by it, but that's how the sun came to be in the sky.

CPSIA information can be obtained
at www.ICGtesting.com
Printed in the USA
LVXC02n2034151213
365414LV00018B/208